PINE VALLEY ponies

THE FORBIDDEN TRAIL

For Pattie Hudson and her late father, Mr Gibbs, who, along with their ranch, staff and amazing horses and ponies, are the inspiration for this series—KW

Scholastic Press
345 Pacific Highway Lindfield NSW 2070
An imprint of Scholastic Australia Pty Limited
PO Box 579 Gosford NSW 2250
ABN 11 000 614 577
www.scholastic.com.au

Part of the Scholastic Group
Sydney • Auckland • New York • Toronto • London • Mexico City
• New Delhi • Hong Kong • Buenos Aires • Puerto Rico

Published by Scholastic Australia in 2015.
Text copyright © Kate Welshman, 2015.
Illustrations by Heath McKenzie, copyright © Scholastic Australia, 2015.
Map on page vi by Keisha Galbraith, copyright © Scholastic Australia, 2015.
Internal photography: riding equipment illustrations © Olga Zakharova | Shutterstock.com.

National Library of Australia Cataloguing-in-Publication entry:
Creator: Welshman, Kate, author.
Title: The forbidden trail / Kate Welshman; Heath McKenzie, illustrator.
ISBN: 9781743624302 (paperback)
Series: Welshman, Kate. Pine Valley ponies; 1.
Target Audience: For primary school age.
Subjects: Ponies—Juvenile fiction.
Horses—Juvenile fiction.
Horsemanship—Juvenile fiction
Other Creators/Contributors:
McKenzie, Heath, illustrator.
Dewey Number: A823.4

Typeset in ITC Stone Serif with Candy Randy.

Printed in China by RR Donnelley.

Scholastic Australia's policy, in association with RR Donnelley, is to use papers that are
renewable and made efficiently from wood grown in responsibly managed forests, so as to
minimise its environmental footprint.

10 9 8 7 6 5 4 3 2 1   15 16 17 18 19 / 1

THE
FORBIDDEN TRAIL

KATE WELSHMAN
Illustrated by HEATH MCKENZIE

A Scholastic Press book
from Scholastic Australia

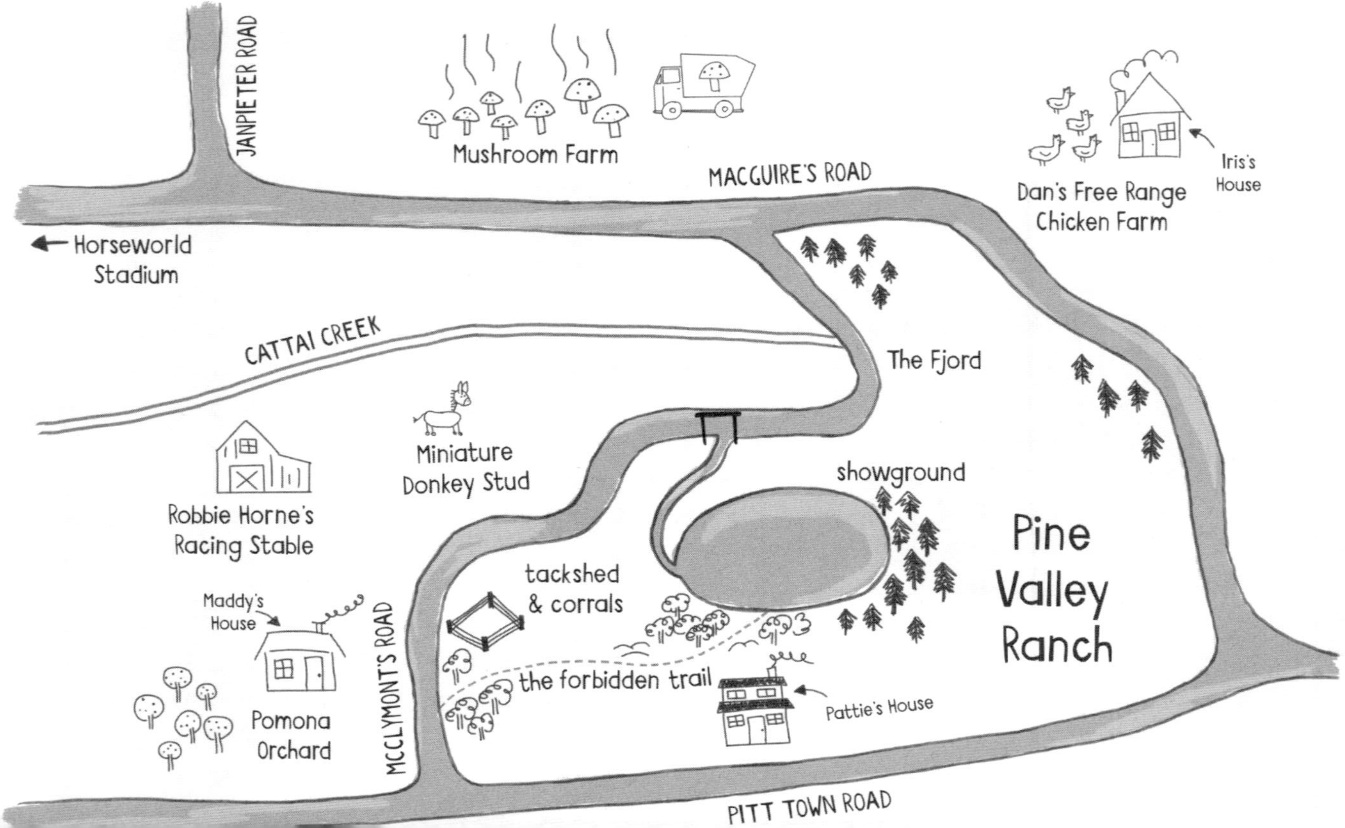
JANPIETER ROAD
Mushroom Farm
MACGUIRE'S ROAD
Dan's Free Range Chicken Farm
Iris's House
Horseworld Stadium
CATTAI CREEK
The Fjord
Miniature Donkey Stud
Robbie Horne's Racing Stable
showground
Pine Valley Ranch
tackshed & corrals
Maddy's House
MCCLYMONT'S ROAD
the forbidden trail
Pattie's House
Pomona Orchard
PITT TOWN ROAD

Chapter 1
Finally Here!

Maddy looked down at her pony's mane as they walked along dusty McClymont's Road. It was the **whitest** mane she'd ever seen.

'That purple shampoo really worked, Snowy,' she told her pony.

Snowy's ears flicked back and he tossed his head.

Maddy giggled. 'What's wrong? You didn't like it?'

Snowy hated being washed, and this morning Maddy had given him the **longest wash** of his life. Her mum had bought a bottle of fancy purple shampoo from the local saddlery. It was meant to be good for getting grey ponies clean—and it was! Snowy was as clean and fresh as a **cotton ball**.

Normally, Maddy didn't mind if Snowy was a bit grubby, but this was no normal day. Today was a day she'd been looking forward to since Christmas. It was the day of her very first riding lesson at **Pine Valley Ranch**!

Maddy could already ride pretty well. She'd had Snowy for a few months now. Mum had taught her a bit, Snowy had taught her a bit and she'd learned a lot from reading the piles of **pony magazines** and **horse books** she kept in her room.

'But you still need proper lessons,' Mum had said on Christmas morning. And then Maddy had unwrapped the voucher for **five** riding lessons.

Pine Valley Ranch was a 150-acre riding ranch, not far from Pomona Orchard, where Maddy lived with her parents and her little brother, Richie. It was owned by the Gibbs family, who'd been teaching horse riding for more than forty years. Even Mum had learned to ride there when she'd been Maddy's age.

Maddy couldn't imagine her

mother being nine years old. It seemed **impossible**.

Maddy leaned back in the saddle as the road grew steeper. If she leaned forward onto the pony's neck as they walked downhill, he might lose his balance.

Snowy was **concentrating**, too. Ears pricked, he took short, careful steps until the road flattened out and the valley rolled open before them.

When they reached the big open gate with the faded 'Pine Valley Ranch' sign hanging above it, Maddy's heart started **thumping** as she dismounted. She wasn't sure whether she was excited or nervous, but it didn't matter. She had driven past this gate with Mum so many times and had imagined the prancing ponies and their happy riders inside. But this time, she was walking right **through** the gate, heading in for her very own riding lessons. They were **finally here**!

Chapter 2

Marjorie's Daughter

'Are you here for the ten o'clock lesson with Pattie?' came a friendly voice from the doorway of the tack shed.

Maddy turned. She was leading Snowy around, unsure what to do. A girl with long, dark hair stood there. She looked about 15.

'I **think** so,' said Maddy, pulling out the crumpled voucher from the pocket of her jeans. She handed it to the girl.

'You must be Marjorie's daughter,' the girl said, looking quickly at the voucher and handing it back. 'My name's Nicole. I'm Pattie's niece. I think Pattie and your mum used to ride together.'

'Mum used to ride a horse called **Brandy**,' said Maddy.

'We still have Brandy! Can you believe it?' Nicole pointed to a dark chestnut horse behind a rail at the side of the shed.

The horse looked old and small, nothing like the **magnificent** animal Maddy imagined when Mum told her stories about her days at Pine Valley Ranch.

'Your lesson's about to start,' said Nicole. 'You'd better go and wait under the big pine tree with the others.'

'So . . .' began Maddy uncertainly, 'do most of the kids here have their own horses?'

'No, you're one of the lucky ones,' Nicole replied. 'Most people here ride the Pine Valley horses. It's not the same as having your own, but it's the **next best thing**.'

Snowy gave Maddy a nudge in the back with his nose, as if to say, 'Come on, get a move on!'

'Okay, okay, Snowy,' said Maddy, running her hand down his silky mane. She led him towards a small group of girls around her age who were standing in the shade of a huge old pine tree. The moment she saw them, her heart sank. They were all wearing special riding pants called **jodhpurs** and **shiny leather ankle boots**. A girl with a glossy black pony even had matching **gloves** and **helmet cover**. She was the one who noticed Maddy first.

'This is the *intermediate* class,' she said with a flick of her long, blonde ponytail. 'Sorry, you've missed the beginner class,' she added, but she didn't sound sorry at all.

'I'm in the ten o'clock class,' said Maddy. 'With Pattie.'

'The intermediate class is for people who can *already* ride,' the girl explained as if Maddy didn't understand her. She raised her eyebrows as she stared at Maddy's gumboots and tatty jeans. Then she looked up at Maddy's helmet. 'Your helmet is **so old**. I bet it doesn't meet safety standards.'

'It used to be my mum's,' replied Maddy. She felt like she might burst into tears.

'This pony has such a sweet face,' said one of the other girls in the group. She was looking at **Snowy**. 'Is he yours?'

The girl with the blonde ponytail scoffed loudly.

'As if *that* pony would ever belong to Pine Valley Ranch.'

The other girl reached out and stroked Snowy's nose. 'He looks pretty nice to me.'

'Hmph!' scoffed the girl with the
ponytail. 'He's not even wearing
horseshoes. That's cruel!'

Maddy looked down at Snowy's
little black hooves. Was the girl right?
Was it cruel not to have horseshoes?
She was beginning to think that
coming to Pine Valley Ranch had
been a **huge mistake**, but then
her thoughts were interrupted by a
woman coming down the hill towards

them. She was followed by three big German Shepherds. Maddy knew right away that the woman was **Pattie**. She'd heard about the three big dogs from Snowy's vet, Hugh Parry. Their names were **Sam**, **Kate** and **Nicks**.

'Come on, girls. On your horses,' Pattie said in a gruff voice.

Maddy had also heard that Pattie could be very strict.

While the girls were mounting

their ponies and adjusting their stirrups, Pattie did a head count.

'There are meant to be **six riders** in this lesson and there are **only five** of you here. Who's missing?'

'It's Iris,' said the girl with the ponytail. 'Late again.'

'Thank you, **Alita**,' said Pattie. 'We'll have to start without her.'

Pattie untied a large bay horse from the rail beside the tack shed. His coat was shiny and he had a white star on his forehead and a triangular snip on his nose. Maddy thought he was the most **beautiful** horse she'd ever seen. Pattie led him away from the shed and mounted swiftly.

'What's his name?' Maddy asked.

'This is **Rey-Del**,' said Pattie as the dogs circled Rey-Del's legs. 'Are you Marjorie's daughter?' she asked, spinning the big, handsome horse around to face Maddy.

Maddy felt strange being thought of as 'Marjorie's daughter', but she nodded anyway.

'I used to ride with your mother,' said Pattie. 'She was **a gutsy rider**!'

Maddy smiled. She felt proud of her mum and could picture her and Pattie galloping across the paddock together as girls.

Maybe someday someone would call her **a gutsy rider**, too.

Chapter 3

That's Horse Riding

Pattie led the class to the showground—a large, flat, grassy area where most of the lessons were taught. There were tall pine trees around the edges. Behind the pine trees was thick bush and a steep, rocky hill that led up to the road. Maddy remembered Mum talking about a **secret shortcut** between the road and the showground that only a few people knew about. But Mum hadn't ridden at Pine Valley for twenty years, so the shortcut was probably overgrown now.

Pattie asked the girls to ride around her in a large circle. 'Don't let your pony get too close to the pony in front of you,' she told them. 'Maddy, get that pony stepping out properly. He's **plodding**.'

Maddy closed her heels around Snowy's sides, but he didn't seem to even feel them. He went on at the same pace.

Before long, Alita **overtook** Maddy on the outside.

'*Of course* he can't walk,' she said under her breath as she came up beside Maddy. 'His feet are bare. How would you feel walking around outside with no shoes on?'

Maddy felt her cheeks burn red.

She was just about to tell Pattie that she wanted to go home when a **loud crack** came from the bush behind the pine trees. Everyone spun around to see what it was. Pattie's

dogs barked and growled.

There was another **loud crack**, then some rustling and a white-and-yellow **flash**. An ancient, dusty palomino pony burst from between the pine branches and **skidded** to a halt just in front of Pattie. Little clouds of dust rose from his hooves.

He must have come down the secret shortcut Mum had told Maddy about!

'Sorry I'm late,' said the palomino's rider, a girl about eight or nine years old with **curly**, straw-coloured hair sticking out of her helmet in every direction.

Maddy grinned. The girl didn't sound very sorry at all!

Pattie wasn't amused. 'Iris Digby!' she snapped. 'You know you're not allowed to ride down that trail. It's forbidden. And do you know *why* it is forbidden, Iris?'

'Because it's . . . um . . . dangerous,' replied the girl, picking **twigs** out of her hair. Her pony seemed to have a whole tree's worth of leaves stuck in his tail.

'Iris, I'm serious,' warned Pattie. 'That trail is for advanced, older riders, in emergencies only. If I catch you on that trail again, I'm going to have to ban you from Pine Valley.'

Iris **gulped**. 'Sorry, Pattie.'

They started the lesson again and Maddy rode behind Iris. She noticed that Iris was wearing jeans, not jodhpurs, and her scuffed white helmet had the words **'EAT MY DUST'** written on the back of it.

Next, the whole class began trotting in a big circle. Maddy saw that Iris was standing up and down in the stirrups to the beat of the trot. This, Mum had told her, was called 'rising to the trot'. Riders did it so they didn't bounce on their horse's back. Maddy could do it—sort of— but not for long stretches.

Soon enough, Pattie noticed that Maddy kept falling out of rhythm.

'Maddy,' she called. 'You mustn't stop rising. I want you to say it aloud, **"up, down, up, down, up, down"** and don't stop.'

'I'm not used to trotting for this

long,' panted Maddy.

'Well, you'll have to get used to it,' said Pattie. 'Learning to ride is hard.'

Maddy tried to do what she'd been told. '**Up, down, up, down, up, down . . .**' she said over and over to herself. After a while, it actually seemed to work. She wasn't bouncing nearly as much.

'Keep trotting,' ordered Pattie, 'and starting with **Alita and QC**, I want each of you to ride a large circle to the outside, one at a time.'

Maddy watched as Alita turned QC, her glossy black horse, to the left and looped around before joining the group again. She slotted in between Iris and Maddy, flicking QC on the shoulder with her crop.

'Your circle was fantastic, Alita,' said Pattie, 'but you didn't need to tap him with your crop. Always use your legs first. Crops are a last resort.'

Iris and her pony made more of an oblong than a circle, and the old palomino leaned to the inside like a racing motorbike.

'Much too fast, Iris!' said Pattie. 'Circles don't have corners. Next time, don't let **Monty** rush. And keep your leg against his side so he doesn't lean in like that.'

Soon it was Maddy's turn. Her circle started badly and just got **worse**. First, Snowy didn't want to leave the group. Maddy had to haul him to the left with all her might. Then she lost her balance and her feet fell out of the stirrups, so she couldn't rise to the trot. Her bottom started **bouncing** on the saddle and soon her hands were bouncing, too. To stop herself falling off, she had to hold onto the **pommel** at the front of the saddle . . . and then Snowy ground to a halt and started picking at a patch of clover.

Maddy heard a tinkling laugh coming from the group. She didn't need to look to know that it was coming from Alita.

Pattie rode over on Rey-Del. Maddy braced herself, but Pattie's voice was kind.

'Come on, Maddy, put your feet back in the stirrups,' she said. 'It's hard to get them back when you're trotting.'

As Maddy was following Pattie's instructions, she wondered whether Snowy had stopped trotting because his feet were sore.

'Snowy doesn't wear horseshoes,' said Maddy in a small voice.

'I hadn't noticed,' replied Pattie.

'Do you think that's the reason he stopped trotting just now? Maybe he has sore feet.'

Pattie shook her head. 'He stopped trotting because you stopped asking him to. How was he to know what to do while your hands and legs were **flapping** around?'

'Alita says it's cruel not to put horseshoes on your pony.'

'That's **rhubarb**,' said Pattie with a chuckle. 'A lot of ponies don't need

need horseshoes. They do just fine barefoot because they have small, tough hooves.'

Maddy was relieved. She tried the circle again. This time it was better. She only lost one stirrup, which she managed to find again without looking down, and Snowy kept trotting for the **whole circle**.

'It's harder than it looks,' said Iris.

'That's horse riding for you,' agreed Pattie.

Chapter 4

New Friends

'Tell us all about the lesson,' said Dad at the dinner table that night.

'Did you fall off?' asked Richie, Maddy's seven-year-old brother. He always asked her that.

'No, I did *not* fall off,' replied Maddy. 'The lesson was fine.'

Mum looked worried. 'Just fine?'

Maddy **shrugged**.

'Was Snowy naughty?' asked Mum.

'Snowy was fine. It's just . . .' Maddy sighed. How could she say how she felt without sounding ungrateful for the riding lesson?

Now both her parents were staring at her.

'I just wasn't as good as the other girls,' she blurted. 'I kept losing my stirrups. And sometimes Snowy wouldn't do what I wanted him to do . . . I'm not sure I want to go back.'

Mum put down her knife and fork. 'Maddy,' she began, 'it sounds like you **need** to keep going back. At least for a few more lessons.'

'Mum's right,' said Dad. 'You can't expect to be the best rider in the class on your very first day.'

'It's not just that,' Maddy explained. 'Everyone knows I'm **"Marjorie's daughter"**. They're expecting me to be as good as Mum.'

'Oh, Maddy!' laughed Mum, putting her hand over Maddy's. 'You're going to be a much more capable rider than I ever was. You should have seen me and **Brandy** on our first day! I accidentally rode her under a tree branch and ended up on the ground looking up at the sky! I bet nothing like that happened to you and Snowy today.'

Mum was right, but Maddy still wasn't sure. 'I don't have the right clothes, either. Almost everyone else has jodhpurs and **special riding boots**.'

'Now, now,' said Dad seriously. 'We're not going to buy expensive riding clothes until we're sure you're going to keep riding. You understand, don't you?'

Maddy nodded.

'Why are you whining, Maddy?' asked Richie, his mouth full of **Churning spaghetti**. 'You get everything you want. You got

a pony for your birthday. You got riding lessons for Christmas. I got a worm farm and a beach towel.' Then he turned to Dad with a cheeky grin on his face. 'I'm *still* waiting for my **motorbike** to arrive.'

'I'm still waiting for your table manners to arrive,' joked Dad.

Maddy folded her arms and gave her brother a grumpy look. But she couldn't think of anything to say back to him because she knew Richie was right.

That week, Maddy rode Snowy almost **every day** after school. She was determined that their trot circles were going to be better at their next lesson. Maybe they wouldn't be as smooth as Alita's and QC's, but still . . . it was something to aim for.

She rode Snowy in the orchard while Dad was pruning the peach trees. She steered him in and out and around and around the trees, trying to keep her balance—and her stirrups! She even practised things she could already do, like going straight from a **halt** to a **trot**, and back again.

Later in the week, Maddy took Snowy out for a slow **trail ride**. It was time to do something **relaxing** together. He'd worked hard with her since the lesson at Pine Valley Ranch. She didn't want him getting bored.

They set out on McClymont's Road, riding on a track next to the road, past the miniature donkey farm, then over a steep, grassy verge where Snowy always snatched a **milk thistle** or two. Snowy broke into a slow trot as they passed the paddock where the racehorse trainer, Robbie Horne, galloped his horses to get them fit. Then they **jig-jogged** to Maguire's Road, Snowy's pink nose snorting happily all the way.

They'd almost reached the chicken farm when Maddy spotted another horse further ahead. It was **cantering** towards them. It was Monty and Iris!

Maddy waved. 'Hi, Iris!'

Iris pulled Monty's reins, bringing him to a stop. Her blonde hair was escaping from the edges of her helmet again.

'Hi! Sorry, I forgot your name, but I know your pony's called Snowy.'

'I'm Maddy. Do you live around here?' Maddy asked.

'I live on the chicken farm,' said Iris, pointing to the hill behind them. 'What about you?'

'I live on the **orchard** on McClymont's Road.'

Snowy and Monty seemed to be introducing themselves, too. Their noses were almost touching. They were sniffing and blowing into each other's nostrils.

'That's how they say **hello**,'

explained Iris. 'They're getting to know each other. See?'

Monty must have decided that Snowy was a cheeky young **whippersnapper**, because all of a sudden he flattened his ears back and lunged at Snowy. Maddy shrieked. Snowy squealed, his eyes rolling in surprise as Monty reached

for his neck.

'Stop him!' Maddy cried.

Iris acted quickly, hauling Monty away and giving him a hard nudge in the ribs with her feet. He lowered his head and gave Snowy a dirty look.

'You **cranky old man!**' she shrieked at Monty.

Maddy dismounted to check on Snowy, but the only thing on his neck was a string of spit.

'It's okay. I don't think he's hurt.'

'Oh, you don't need to worry about that,' said Iris. 'Monty doesn't have any teeth. He lost the last one about five years ago. He's nearly **forty**, you know.'

'Snowy's only **six**. I didn't know horses lived that long. Forty—wow!'

Iris shrugged. 'It must be something in the hay.'

Maddy flicked the spit off Snowy's neck and climbed back on. 'How does Monty eat hay or grass if he has no teeth?' she asked.

'Well . . . he doesn't eat much hay. Mostly he gets wet chaff, which is hay chopped up into tiny pieces. And he can't eat his pellets unless we wet them and mash them up.'

'Has he always been this cranky?'

Iris thought for a while. 'Yeah,' she admitted, 'but he's got **a lot of heart**. He was just putting Snowy in his place.' She patted Monty's neck lovingly. Monty craned his head around and licked her boot with his thick, pink tongue.

Maddy smiled. She decided she liked Iris a lot. And Monty, too. The old grouch did have a **big heart**.

The girls rode back towards McClymont's Road together, a safe distance apart. They chattered all the way. Monty stuck his ears back and pulled faces. Snowy wrinkled his nose.

As they turned onto McClymont's Road, Iris pointed to an old fence post hidden in the bush at the side of the road.

'See that post?' she said in a voice so soft it was almost a whisper. 'That **marks the trail**.'

'What trail?' Maddy asked in a normal voice.

'The trail to Pine Valley Ranch.'

'Oh . . .' Maddy remembered how

angry Pattie had sounded when Iris had ridden down the trail before their lesson last week.

'I ride on it all the time,' said Iris.

'But Pattie says it's forbidden,' replied Maddy.

Iris rolled her eyes.

'She said,' Maddy added, 'that if she catches you on it again, she'll ban you from Pine Valley Ranch.'

'Monty and I can handle that trail *easily*,' Iris said firmly. 'We can even trot down it, no problem.'

Maddy didn't want to argue, but she didn't want Iris to be banned from the ranch, either. She was the only friend she had there.

'I don't want you to leave Pine Valley Ranch,' Maddy said seriously.

'Please promise me you won't go down the forbidden trail again?'

Iris sighed and rolled her eyes again. 'Okay,' she finally agreed.

The girls rode side-by-side all the way back to Maddy's orchard, then Iris spun Monty around and took off up the road at a **gallop**. Monty's thick, white tail streamed out behind him like a banner.

'I hope you still have that much energy when *you're* forty,' Maddy said to Snowy.

Chapter 5

Danger on the Trail

On Saturday morning, Maddy got up early to wash Snowy. She used the special purple shampoo again, rubbing Snowy's coat with the sponge until he was a **ball of purple suds**. She even washed his silky forelock that fell over his forehead and the tips of his pointy little ears.

Snowy wasn't enjoying himself,

not one little bit. Maddy caught him hopefully eyeing a patch of mud next to the shed.

'Don't even *think* about it, Snowy,' she warned, knowing that her pony would get down and **roll in the mud** if she let him. Snowy hated being clean.

'You're just lucky you only have to look nice one day a week,' said Maddy, laughing.

She hosed off all the shampoo and then rubbed Snowy's coat with a big towel. That was the one part of being washed that Snowy seemed to enjoy. He lowered his head so that Maddy could dry his head and ears.

As Maddy sat under a nearby peach tree cleaning her second-hand

saddle and bridle, she wondered
what the other girls in the class were
doing right now. She imagined Iris
already in the saddle, trotting around
her chicken farm to warm up before
the lesson. She imagined Alita still
asleep in bed while someone else
brushed QC's jet-black coat for her.

The other girls in the class didn't
have their own horses. Instead they
rode the Pine Valley horses. They
were perfectly nice horses, but
riding someone else's horse on the
weekend was nothing like having
your own. Maddy imagined those
girls eating their breakfast and
dreaming of a day when they
could look out their bedroom window
and see a pony looking back at

them. That was what had happened to Maddy three months ago when Mum had rescued Snowy from the sale yards. Mum had woken her up on the morning of her ninth birthday and told her to look out the window. Maddy had to rub her eyes to check she wasn't **dreaming**. Standing on the front lawn, picking at the grass and looking around curiously, had been the **cutest, cleverest Welsh pony** in the world— Snowy!

Sometimes Maddy *still* had to tell herself she wasn't dreaming. In quiet moments like this one, when she was just cleaning Snowy's tack and watching him eat hay, she felt like the luckiest girl in the world.

After breakfast, Maddy saddled up and set off down McClymont's Road. It was a warm, foggy morning and Maddy knew it was going to be hot once the fog cleared. She kept Snowy to the grass verge in case any cars came along. They might not see her and Snowy through the **thick, white mist**.

Maddy thought about Iris and whether she would keep her promise to take the long way to Pine Valley Ranch, rather than trotting down the shortcut. Further up the road Maddy could see the fence post that marked the beginning of the **forbidden trail**. It was surrounded by bush

and fog. She'd never noticed it before Iris had pointed it out. Now she couldn't ignore it.

When they reached the post, Maddy brought Snowy to a halt.

'Whoa, there,' she said, noticing how quickly Snowy reacted to her voice. She hardly needed to use the reins at all.

Curious, Maddy turned Snowy off the verge towards the narrow dirt track that weaved between the trees and boulders, then over a ridge. To Maddy, it looked like it led over the edge of a cliff. She felt terrified just looking down there. 'I'd *never* ride you down there,' she told Snowy. 'Not in a million years.'

Snowy pricked his ears and

sniffed the air. Something was wrong and he could smell it.

Maddy tugged on the left rein to turn him around, but only his head and neck turned. His hooves stayed firmly put.

'Come on, Snowy!'

It was then that Maddy heard the **whinny**. At first, she thought she had imagined it, but when Snowy raised his head and whinnied back, she knew there must be a horse down there somewhere.

Was it Monty? Maybe Iris had fallen off and Monty was calling out for help! Maybe one of the Pine Valley horses was lost!

'*Neiiiiiigh!*' came the worried whinny again. Snowy neighed back again.

'Do you know that horse?' Maddy asked Snowy. Then she rode him a little further down the trail.

'Iris?' she called out. 'Is that you?'

'*Help!*' came a voice from further down the trail. It sounded faint—a long way away.

'Iris!' Maddy called again, carefully urging Snowy further along. The track led them to the edge of a big sandstone boulder. Maddy peered down to the track below. She'd never ridden down something **so steep or so big**. When she realised that Snowy wasn't going to stop, she leaned back and shoved her feet forward, loosening the reins so he could stretch out his neck. With a grunt, Snowy dropped off the edge, landing on the track with a jolt that sent Maddy sprawling onto his neck. She sat up, gathered her reins and gave the pony a huge pat.

'Good boy,' she said breathlessly. **'My good, brave boy.'**

Snowy snorted and walked on as if nothing had happened.

They followed the trail around the broad trunks of gum trees, over rocks and through dried-up gullies.

'This isn't so bad,' said Maddy. She'd only just spoken the words when another cry for help rang out.

'*HELP!*'

The cries were growing more frantic. In fact, Maddy was beginning to think it wasn't Iris at all. She couldn't imagine Iris being so . . .

so helpless.

'Who's there?' shouted Maddy, slowly continuing down the trail.

'Who are *you*?' replied a panicked voice, echoing up the trail.

'It's Maddy.'

'*Who*?'

Snowy let out another **whinny**, and after a second or two, another horse whinnied back.

'Come on, Snowy,' Maddy said, urging him into a trot. 'Let's find out who it is.'

They pranced through a stand of bracken before reaching another huge boulder. Maddy leaned back again as Snowy skidded down, taking up trot again once they reached the other side. They came around a corner and finally Maddy saw who was on the trail below.

It was Alita and her beautiful black horse, QC!

Chapter 6

A Gutsy Rider

'What are *you* doing here?' Alita asked grumpily.

'I could ask you the same question,' Maddy replied, easing Snowy back to a walk. She halted him a few metres away from QC. After Monty had tried to take a chunk out of Snowy's neck with his gums, she wasn't willing to get any closer to a strange horse.

QC had stopped on a narrow part

of the trail, right in front of a clump of huge tree roots. He sniffed the tree roots and looked desperately back up at Snowy.

'Well, aren't you going to help?' Alita demanded, folding her arms. 'Can't you see we're *stuck*?'

Maddy looked at QC's legs. They didn't look stuck or caught. 'Why don't you just **turn him around**?' she asked.

'There just isn't enough room,' said Alita. She pointed to the rock wall on one side of her and the gigantic turpentine tree on the other.

'Can't you rein him back?'

'He won't. It's too steep. And he won't go forward either. It's these tree roots . . .' Alita's face was red now. She looked like she was about to cry. 'He's afraid of the tree roots. He won't go over them. He's being so *stupid!*'

Alita threw her reins on QC's neck. 'Stupid horse!'

Maddy had her own opinion about who was being stupid, but she kept it to herself. She could see the tears shining in Alita's eyes, and she felt **sorry** for the girl. Alita looked frustrated and scared. Maddy wondered how long they'd been stuck there.

'And I dropped my riding crop, too!' she cried, tears streaming down her red cheeks. 'Somewhere back there on the trail. I'm going to be in huge trouble with my dad because it cost a lot of money.'

'Don't worry,' Maddy said calmly, 'we'll get you out of here.'

She was surprised how clearly she was thinking as she dismounted Snowy. She walked to QC, bent down and grabbed his reins under his chin, near the bit.

'Let's try to bring him further up the track. There's enough room to turn around up there.'

'Well . . . okay . . .' Alita agreed in a trembling voice.

Maddy pulled on QC's reins and tried to coax him to walk up next to Snowy. She clucked her tongue. 'Come on, QC,' she panted, leaning on the reins, but QC really was stuck. His hooves didn't move.

'It's no use!' wailed Alita, her legs hanging limply by her horse's sweating sides. 'We'll be stuck here forever.'

Maddy sighed and let go of QC's reins. She knew the horse was worried about the tree roots by the way he kept **sniffing** them and **rolling** his eyes. But Alita wasn't helping either. Mum had often told Maddy that horses could sense fear. Alita was adding to QC's fear.

'Alita, why don't you jump off and come up here?' said Maddy.

'What? Why?'

'Just do it,' said Maddy. Alita swung one leg over QC's sleek neck and slithered down his shoulder.

'Leave him there,' said Maddy. 'He's not going anywhere.'

Alita climbed over the tree roots, tripping a few times before reaching Maddy and Snowy.

'Here,' said Maddy, handing her the reins, 'take Snowy further up and wait for me.'

Maddy scrambled over the tree roots down to QC, leaning against the turpentine for balance. With one foot in the stirrup of Alita's expensive saddle and the other braced against the trunk of the tree, Maddy managed to mount QC. For a moment she felt amazing, like a **princess**, but then she remembered she had an important job to do.

Gathering up the reins, she squeezed QC's sides firmly with her heels. She felt him flinch, but he didn't move forward. Maddy **clucked** her tongue and **thudded** her heels against him again. He still wouldn't move a muscle.

'Told you!' Alita called out from further up the hill.

'Oh, please be *quiet*,' Maddy muttered under her breath. Then she decided to try an old trick Mum had taught her in her early days of riding Snowy. She took QC's reins short in one hand, so there was a loop in the end of the reins. With her other hand, she slapped the loop on one side of QC's neck, then the other.

QC didn't know what had hit him. He **shot** forward, scrambling over the scary tree roots with his front

hooves. Then he did a huge leap and Maddy had to grab the horse's silky mane to stay on! He rushed up to Snowy and came to an abrupt **halt**!

Maddy patted his neck gently to let him know he'd done something good.

'You did it!' squealed Alita, suddenly happy. Then, just as quickly, her face fell again and her voice turned into a whine. 'Now we have to go back and get my riding crop! Can you get him to go back over those roots?'

Maddy looked over her shoulder and then back at Alita.

'Why did you bring him down the trail in the first place?' Maddy asked.

Alita looked like she was going to say something nasty, but then she just **shrugged**.

Maddy looked at her watch. It was almost ten o'clock. 'How far is it to the showground from here?'

'Not far,' Alita replied. 'We're pretty close to the bottom of the trail. It'll only take a few minutes to get down. *If* you can get QC back over those tree roots.'

Maddy pulled QC around in a tight circle, so they were facing downhill again. 'I can do it,' she said, realising at last just how tall QC was, and how far she was from the ground. It felt a little scary, but mostly **amazing**. 'Follow me.'

She pointed QC straight for the middle of the clump of roots. When he dropped his head and slowed his step, she nudged his sides and held her hands forward, ready for him to jump over. He hung back for just a moment before **launching** himself —all four hooves in the air at once —over the roots. Maddy landed on the saddle's cantle with a thud, but quickly righted herself.

'There was about a metre of

daylight between your bottom and the saddle just then,' said Alita as she took dainty steps over the roots. Snowy followed her obediently. 'You can really hurt a horse's back by bouncing around like that. You'd better get off him and give him back to me.'

Maddy waited until everyone was safely over the roots before dismounting QC. It was nothing like getting off Snowy, who was only about twelve hands high. QC was closer to **fifteen hands**. She landed on the hard ground with a jolt.

Alita came up behind her and passed her Snowy's reins, snatching QC's back at the same time. Something down the hill caught

Alita's attention.

'My crop! Oh, thank goodness!'

Maddy mounted Snowy, who seemed so small underneath her compared with QC. Still, at least he wasn't scared of something as **silly** as a clump of tree roots. Ahead of her, Alita was mounting, her precious riding crop back in her hand. The two girls rode in silence down the rest of the trail. It ended between two boulders.

As they rode onto the showground, Sam, Kate and even old Nicks barked and bounded up to them. Maddy **gulped**. Pattie was there. They heard her before they saw her.

'Alita Jessup! Maddy Sharpe! What on earth are you doing?'

Chapter 7

Riding in Pairs

Pattie stood in front of them with her hands on her hips and a frown on her face. Her dogs sat at her feet.

'Did I, or did I not, explain the rules about that trail last week?' she sternly asked.

'You did,' Alita said meekly. Maddy was too afraid to speak.

Pattie took a step towards them

and her voice went dangerously low. 'I want a word with both of you after this lesson. I expect a lot more from you two. Especially you, Maddy.'

Maddy looked down at Snowy's silky mane.

The other four girls in the class were lined up under the pine trees. Iris gave Maddy **a cheeky smile**. Maddy was too embarrassed to smile back or explain what she'd been doing on the **forbidden trail**. Pattie took her position in front of the girls and explained what they were going to practise during the lesson.

Maddy was so shaken by what had just happened, both on the trail with Alita and here on the showground with Pattie, that she didn't worry about what she was wearing or whether she was bouncing during the trot. She just concentrated on Snowy and where she was meant to be riding him.

They were practising riding in pairs today. Maddy was relieved when she and Snowy were paired with Iris and Monty. The girls rode as close together as they dared. They managed to stay in a pair as they walked and trotted in a **big loop** and then in smaller circles and even a figure-of-eight.

'Look!' Iris cried excitedly as they trotted together down the long side of the showground. 'Their legs are moving together! Like **dancers!**'

Maddy looked down and saw that

the ponies' front legs were moving
out in sync. For the first time since
she'd set off from home, she smiled.

'Let's keep it up for as long as we
can!' said Iris.

'Everyone look at Maddy and Iris,'
Pattie called out. 'If those ponies
were the same colour, they'd win
the **pair of ponies** class at the
Sydney Royal Easter Show!'

Maddy and Iris broke into huge

grins, but Monty, who knew that his rider was distracted, nipped at Snowy with his gums. Iris started laughing and soon the ponies were veering off in different directions.

'Oh dear,' said Pattie with a chuckle. 'I spoke too soon. At this rate, you'll be lucky to place at the Pine Valley Gymkhana in May. Forget about the **Easter Show!**'

'There's going to be a gymkhana

here in May?' Maddy asked Iris eagerly, once they'd managed to line up their ponies again.

'There are two every year,' chirped Iris. 'At the last gymkhana, Monty and I won the barrel racing and the bending. It was heaps of fun!'

Maddy hoped she'd be able to go to the next gymkhana.

After the lesson, Maddy and Alita stayed back to talk to Pattie. Maddy couldn't believe how smug Alita looked. She had a little smile on her face, as if she'd just heard a joke that no-one else could understand.

'So what were you two doing on the trail this morning?' Pattie asked.

Maddy wanted Pattie to know that she'd only ridden on the trail to help

Alita, but Alita was silent. She just had that silly, snooty smile on her face and looked nastily at Maddy.

Pattie put her hands on her hips. 'Well? I'm waiting.'

'I'm sorry,' said Maddy. 'I'll never do it again. I . . . I rode down there to help Alita.'

Alita huffed and rolled her eyes. 'Don't blame me, Maddy.' She turned to Pattie. 'I dropped my riding crop at the beginning of the trail and then I couldn't turn around. I didn't realise it was so **dangerous**.'

'Well, I hope you've realised now.'

Both girls nodded.

'To make it up to me, I'd like you two to sweep out the tack shed.'

Alita was shocked. 'What? Like,

right *now*?'

Pattie nodded.

'But I have to get measured for my new **ballet** costume,' said Alita.

'Then you'd better hurry to the shed and get it over and done with,' Pattie replied. 'Off you go. I have another class to teach.'

'Sorry, Pattie,' Maddy repeated. She rode after Alita towards the tack shed, feeling quite sick. What would Pattie think of her now?

Chapter 8

You Wouldn't Believe It!

Alita's mother, Mrs Jessup, was
waiting at the tack shed when
the girls arrived. She was wearing a
black jumpsuit with silver high heels.
She looked quite out of place on the
dusty ranch.

'Chop chop, Alita,' she called,
waving around her handbag to get
Alita's attention. QC took one look
at her and **spooked**, leaping

suddenly to the side.

'*Mu-um* . . .' whined Alita.

Mrs Jessup peered at her daughter over the rims of her sunglasses. 'We have to be in the city in half an hour for your measuring.'

'I know, but Pattie says I have to **sweep out the shed**.'

'Whatever for?' asked Mrs Jessup, but she didn't wait for an answer. 'Get one of the grooms to do it. That's what we pay for, isn't it?'

Mrs Jessup yanked QC's reins out of Alita's hand and shook them **briskly** at Maddy.

'Would you take my daughter's horse, please?'

'I'll take him,' came a familiar voice. Iris came out of the tack shed, taking off her helmet. Her blonde curls were **bouncing** on her shoulders. She took the reins from Mrs Jessup.

Alita and her mother left without another word. Maddy shook her head. 'That girl is **unbelievable**,' she said.

Iris laughed. 'Well, now you can see where she gets it from.'

'She got me into trouble with Pattie,' Maddy explained, her voice trembling a little. 'I was only trying to help and now I don't think Pattie likes me anymore.'

'Because you rode down **the forbidden trail**?'

Maddy nodded.

'Oh, don't worry about that. Pattie doesn't hold grudges. Next weekend, she will have forgotten about it.'

'Really?'

Iris nodded and Maddy felt much better.

'Let's tie these guys in the corrals,' said Iris.

The girls led the horses into the small yards where the horses could be tied up, fed and groomed, apart from each other. Monty was already tied up and **munching** on something sloppy.

'I love it when Alita leaves without looking after QC,' Iris admitted. 'It means I get to rub him down.'

'Do you think you could help me sweep out the tack shed after that?' Maddy asked. 'It's my punishment for riding on the trail. Alita's too, but . . .'

Iris grinned. 'Sure. And after that we'll go up to the dining room.'

Maddy didn't know what she was talking about. 'Dining room?'

'Yeah. That building on the hill. That's where Mr Gibbs serves tea on the weekend. He's Pattie's dad. Today he's making pikelets with **jam and cream**. My favourite!'

The girls unsaddled and rubbed down Snowy and QC. Then they fixed them some hay nets. When they were sure the horses were settled, they grabbed some straw brooms and started sweeping out the shed. It was big and dirty, and by the time they'd finished, Maddy felt like she could eat about a **thousand** pikelets.

The dining hall was a huge room

with a long counter and a few tables and chairs. There were windows along one side and you could see onto the paddocks.

As the girls walked in, an old man in an apron came to the serving counter. 'Look who's here!' he said. 'It's that **Cheeky** Iris Digby.'

'Hi, Mr Gibbs,' chirped Iris.

Mr Gibbs looked at Maddy. He narrowed his eyes and twirled the edge of his grey moustache. He looked like he was trying to figure something out.

'Are you Marjorie's daughter?' he finally asked.

'Yes,' Maddy said in a small voice.

'Your mother came to my riding camps every year for more than a decade,' said Mr Gibbs. 'You look exactly like her.'

Maddy smiled and shrugged. After her big adventure on the forbidden trail, though, she thought she might live up to her mum's plucky riding after all. She knew she'd helped Alita and QC out of a dangerous pickle. When she thought about it, her chest **puffed out** with pride.

Iris sniffed the air. 'Are those pikelets ready yet?' she asked hopefully.

'Sit down, sit down,' said Mr Gibbs. 'I'll bring them right out. And a pot of tea, too?'

'Yes, please!' said Iris, leading Maddy to a table by the windows.

The girls made themselves

comfortable and soon Mr Gibbs was walking out of the kitchen with a tray of tea and pikelets.

'I don't want to see a crumb left!' he announced before returning to the kitchen.

Iris took a huge bite out of a pikelet that left a **dollop of cream** on her nose. Then she poured them both cups of tea.

Maddy heaped lots of milk and sugar into her tea and took a big hot gulp.

Iris leaned in and whispered. 'So tell me why you were *really* on that trail.'

Maddy swallowed a mouthful of tea and took a deep breath. 'You wouldn't **believe** it,' she began, and told her new friend all about it.

Pattie may never know the full story, Maddy thought to herself, but it was good to know she had a friend on her side. Perhaps lessons at Pine Valley Ranch wouldn't be so bad after all!

PINE VALLEY RANCH

PONY
Profiles

PINE VALLEY RANCH

Name: Snowy

Owner: Maddy

Home: Pomona Orchard

Colour: Grey

Gender: Gelding

Breed: Part-Welsh

Height: 12 hands

Age: 6

Favourite food: Milk thistles

Favourite activity: Rolling in mud

PINE VALLEY RANCH

Name: Monty

Owner: Iris

Home: Dan's Free Range Chicken Farm

Colour: Palomino

Gender: Gelding

Breed: Quarter horse

Height: 13 hands 3 inches

Age: 38

Favourite food: Bran mash

Favourite activity: Barrel racing

PINE VALLEY RANCH

Name: QC

Owner: Alita

Home: Pine Valley Ranch

Colour: Black

Gender: Gelding

Breed: Stock horse cross English Riding Pony

Height: 14 hands 3 inches

Age: 13

Favourite food: Rolled oats

Favourite activity: Being groomed

PINE VALLEY RANCH

Name: Rey-Del

Owner: Gibbs Family

Home: Pine Valley Ranch

Colour: Bay, with a star and snip

Gender: Gelding

Breed: Quarter horse

Height: 15 hands 1 inch

Age: 9

Favourite food: Bran pellets

Favourite activity: Playing with Pattie's dogs

Some Horsy Q & A

How do you measure a pony?

A pony is measured from the bottom of his front hoof to the top of the highest part of his back (withers). Horses are measured in 'hands'. One hand is equal to four inches, or 10 centimetres. So Snowy measures 1.2 metres from his hoof to his withers.

Why do you call Snowy 'grey' when he's actually white?

Snowy, although almost all the hairs in his coat are white, would have been grey when he was younger. He also has black skin. Truly white horses are born white and have pink skin.

How long do ponies live?

Ponies have a lifespan of 25–30 years. However, some ponies, like Monty, can live into their forties and beyond.

Maddy's Glossary

Cantle: The raised, curved part at the back of a horse's saddle.

Chaff: Hay that has been chopped into short lengths.

Crop: A short, flexible whip with a loop for the hand, used when riding horses.

Gymkhana: A daytime event involving races and competitions on horseback, usually for children.

Hay: Grass that has been mown and dried out for use as animal food.

Jodhpurs: Long, close-fitting pants worn for horse riding.

Pommel: The upward-curving part of the saddle in front of the rider, used for mounting and holding on.

Rising to the trot: Also known as 'posting to the trot', the rider rises from the saddle with every second beat of the trot.

Stirrups: A pair of loops with flat bases, usually metal, attached to either side of the saddle to support the rider's foot.

Tack: A piece of equipment put on a horse, for example, saddles, bridles, halters and harnesses.

Tack shed: A building that stores tack to keep it away from the weather and vermin, like rats and mice.

Catch
Maddy and Snowy
in their next pony
adventure!

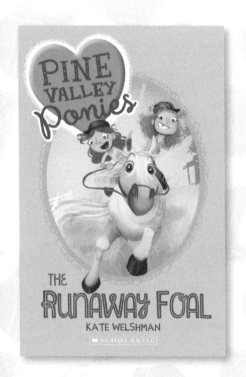

THE
RUNAWAY
FOAL
Out now!